Little Black Girl

*Oh, the Things
You Can Do!*

Dedicated to my nan, Nellie Brandy,

to my mum and to my nieces.

–K.H.B.

Nancy Paulsen Books

An imprint of Penguin Random House LLC, New York

First published in the United States of America by Nancy Paulsen Books,
an imprint of Penguin Random House LLC, 2022

Copyright © 2022 by Kirby Howell-Baptiste

Visit us online at penguinrandomhouse.com

Library of Congress Cataloging-in-Publication Data
Names: Howell-Baptiste, Kirby, author. | Davey, Paul, illustrator.
Title: Little Black girl / Kirby Howell-Baptiste; illustrated by Paul Davey.
Description: New York: Nancy Paulsen Books, 2022. | Summary: "A little Black girl confidently
and joyously pursues her dream of robotics"–Provided by publisher.
Identifiers: LCCN 2022011448 (print) | LCCN 2022011449 (ebook) | ISBN 9780593406236 (hardcover) |
ISBN 9780593406250 (kindle edition) | ISBN 9780593406243 (epub)
Subjects: CYAC: Stories in rhyme. | Self-confidence–Fiction. | African Americans–Fiction. |
LCGFT: Picture books. | Stories in rhyme.
Classification: LCC PZ8.3.H8379 Li 2022 (print) | LCC PZ8.3.H8379 (ebook) | DDC [E]–dc23
LC record available at https://lccn.loc.gov/2022011448
LC ebook record available at https://lccn.loc.gov/2022011449

Printed in the United States of America

ISBN 9780593406236
1 3 5 7 9 10 8 6 4 2
PC

Edited by Stacey Barney | Art direction by Cecilia Yung
Design by Eileen Savage | Text set in Intro
The art was done digitally in Clip Studio Paint and Procreate.

Little Black Girl

Oh, the Things You Can Do!

KIRBY HOWELL-BAPTISTE

illustrated by **PAUL DAVEY**

 Nancy Paulsen Books

Little Black Girl, oh, the things you can do.

Did anyone mention the world's open to you?

You have sparks in your brain and fire in your heart.

You can decide where to stop and where to start.

You were born unique. None of us are the same.

Your only job: Make them remember your name.

"I want to be an engineer!"

"Boo!" they may say,

but don't let the naysayers get in your way.

A writer, a vet, a movie director,
a poet, a coder, a fossil collector.

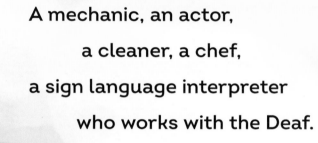

A mechanic, an actor,
    a cleaner, a chef,
a sign language interpreter
    who works with the Deaf.

An astronaut, a yogi,

a potter, a queen,

a cosplayer, a nerd,

a comedian, the dean.

There's no character, no type, no mold you must fit,
no shrinking or hiding or diminishing your wit.

Cherish your youth, take the time that you need
to grow and to flourish a plant from a seed.

Do what you want, the world's a blank slate,

and remember that love will always destroy hate.

You can travel the world or stay close to home.

The world is your oyster, to wander and roam.

Claudette Colvin

Audre Lorde

Toni Morrison

No "She's too Black" or "Not Black enough,"

words you may hear, but your skin will grow tough.

Florence
Griffith
Joyner

Hattie
McDaniel

Joy
Buolamwini

Not tough on your own, for there are many others,
generations of women, your sisters and mothers.

For we are Black women who have weathered the storm.

When the world is cold, we keep each other warm.

Our history is rich, we've been here since the start,
growing and changing, a living work of art.

Our presence is a gift, each better than the last.

Moment by moment, we are writing the past.

Our future is vast. You'll shatter the ceiling,
bring others with you to share that great feeling.

There are magical things just waiting for you.

Little Black Girl, oh, the things you can do!